DINK, JOSH, AND RUTH ROSE AREN'T THE
ONLY KID DETECTIVES!

WHAT ABOUT YOU?

CAN YOU FIND THE HIDDEN MESSAGE
INSIDE THIS BOOK?

There are 26 illustrations in this
book, not counting the one on the title
page, the map at the beginning, and the
picture of art supplies that repeats at the
start of many of the chapters. In each of
the 26 illustrations, there's a hidden letter. If you can find all the letters, you will
spell out a secret message!

If you're stumped, the answer is on
the bottom of page 133.

HAPPY DETECTING!

I dedicate this book to teachers, parents, and grandparents
who put books into the hands of children.
—R.R.

To Bryce DePari, a champion A to Z reader!
—J.S.G.

Text copyright © 2021 by Ron Roy
Cover art copyright © 2021 by Stephen Gilpin
Interior illustrations copyright © 2021 by John Steven Gurney

Visit us on the Web!
rhcbooks.com

Educators and librarians, for a variety of teaching tools,
visit us at RHTeachersLibrarians.com

Library of Congress Cataloging-in-Publication Data
Names: Roy, Ron, author. | Gurney, John Steven, illustrator.
Title: Crime in the crypt / by Ron Roy; illustrated by John Steven Gurney.
Description: New York: Random House Children's Books, [2021] |
Series: A to Z mysteries. Super edition; #13 | "A Stepping Stone book." |
Summary: "When Ruth Rose's grandmother is accused of stealing, it's up
to Dink, Josh, and Ruth Rose to clear her name." —Provided by publisher.
Identifiers: LCCN 2020032680 (print) | LCCN 2020032681 (ebook) |
ISBN 978-0-593-30181-4 (trade paperback) | ISBN 978-0-593-30182-1 (library binding) |
ISBN 978-0-593-30183-8 (ebook)
Subjects: CYAC: Robbers and outlaws—Fiction. | Cemeteries—Fiction. |
Friendship—Fiction. | Brooklyn (New York, N.Y.)—Fiction. | Mystery and
detective stories.
Classification: LCC PZ7.R8139 Cri 2021 (print) | LCC PZ7.R8139 (ebook) |
DDC [Fic]—dc23

Printed in the United States of America
10 9 8 7 6 5 4 3 2 1

This book has been officially leveled by using the F&P Text Level Gradient™
Leveling System.

A to Z Mysteries®

SUPER EDITION 13

Crime in the Crypt

ROYCE

by Ron Roy

illustrated by
John Steven Gurney

A STEPPING STONE BOOK™

Random House   New York

THE BRONX

WELCOME TO

A to Z Mysteries

ON LOCATION IN

BROOKLYN, NY

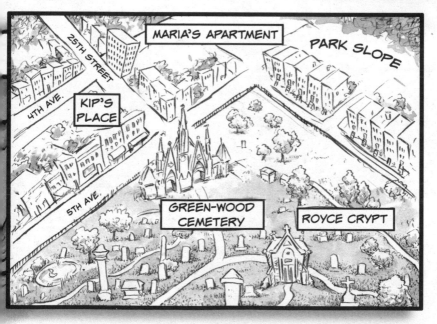

25TH STREET

4TH AVE.

MARIA'S APARTMENT

PARK SLOPE

KIP'S PLACE

5TH AVE.

GREEN-WOOD CEMETERY

ROYCE CRYPT

CHAPTER 1

"OH NO!" Josh moaned. He was asleep, sitting next to Dink on a train. Ruth Rose sat across from them, with her red backpack on the seat next to her. Because she always dressed in one color, she also had a red hoodie, jeans, and headband. A red scarf was draped around her neck.

Josh smacked his lips as if he were tasting something delicious. His eyelids fluttered. He tugged a thread of yarn from the sleeve of his sweater. Ruth Rose reached across and pulled the yarn from Josh's fingers, waking him up.

"What's going on?" Josh croaked.

"You were moaning," Dink told his friend.

"And ruining your sweater," Ruth Rose added.

Josh yawned. "I was having a weird dream," he said.

"Tell us," Dink said. "We love your dreams."

Josh rubbed his eyes, then told Dink and Ruth Rose he dreamed he was in a spaceship made of ice cream. "I was starving, so I nibbled on it," he said. "I kept eating until there was no spaceship left. I began to fall to Earth!"

Dink grinned. "Wait. You ate a *spaceship*?" he asked.

"It was made of *pistachio* ice cream!" Josh said.

The kids were riding the train from Hartford, Connecticut, to New York City. It was early October, and they were going to meet Ruth Rose's grandmother Gram Hathaway. Gram was in New York visiting her best friend, Maria Hoffman.

A conductor in a blue uniform walked up to their seats. "This will be the last stop. Everyone gets off at Grand Central," he said. "Is someone meeting you kids?"

"My grandmother is," Ruth Rose said. She showed the man a letter. "She says to get off the train, walk up a ramp, and she'll be waiting."

The man smiled. "That'll do it," he said. "The ramp will be on your left when you get off. Is this your first time in the city?"

"No," Dink said. "My uncle lives here, and we visited him last year."

The train started to slow. "Have fun in the Big Apple," the man said, and walked to the end of their train car.

"Why do they call New York City the Big Apple?" Josh asked. "Why not the Big Chocolate Chip Cookie?"

Dink grinned. "Or the Big Broccoli?" he said.

The train went into a tunnel. It slowed some more, then stopped.

A voice announced, "GRAND CEN-TRAL TERMINAL . . . LAST STOP. . . . EVERYONE MUST LEAVE THE TRAIN. . . . WATCH YOUR STEP!"

Dink, Josh, and Ruth Rose grabbed their jackets and backpacks and headed for the door, which had swished open. A stream of people left the train. Every-one seemed to be in a hurry. Some of the people dragged suitcases on wheels. Most were talking or texting on cell phones.

The kids found the ramp and fol-lowed the other passengers. They passed recycling bins, where people dropped newspapers, bottles, and cans. A teen-age girl stood on a box, playing a violin. A few people tossed coins and bills into her violin case, which was open near her feet.

"Guys, did you see that?" Josh asked.

"If I learn to play the violin, I can come here and make tons of money!"

Dink laughed. "They'll probably arrest you for noise pollution," he said.

"You're a riot, Wyatt," Josh said.

At the top of the ramp, the kids moved to one side so the rest of the people could keep walking. There were signs everywhere, pointing to taxis, subway stations, and exits.

"Now we wait," Ruth Rose said, turning her head to look for her grandmother.

"How long?" Josh asked. "I'm starving!"

Dink poked him. "You just ate an ice cream spaceship!"

Josh poked him back. "Doesn't count," he said. "I was *dreaming.* In real life, I'm still hungry!"

Just then, a voice called, "RUTH ROSE, OVER HERE!" Gram Hathaway was standing on a bench, waving her hands in the air. The kids zigzagged through the crowd and made their way to the bench. Gram Hathaway hugged each of them.

"Right on time!" Gram said, stepping off the bench. "And you were smart to dress warm. October in New York can get chilly." She was wearing a baseball cap and a fleece vest over a flannel shirt and jeans.

Like Ruth Rose, Dink wore a hooded

sweatshirt and jeans. Josh had on a baggy sweater and cargo pants.

"Follow me!" Gram said, pointing toward an exit. "Brooklyn is that way."

"Are we walking there?" Josh asked.

"No, it's too far," Gram said. "We'll get a taxi." She ushered them out to the street and stepped to the curb, waving for a cab.

CHAPTER 2

A yellow cab pulled up and stopped. Gram opened the rear door, and the kids climbed in with their backpacks. Gram sat next to the driver. He wore a Yankees cap over dreadlocks.

"Can you take us to Park Slope, please?" Gram asked.

"No problem," the man said, easing his cab into the stream of traffic.

"What's Park Slope?" Dink asked.

"It's the neighborhood in Brooklyn where Maria lives," Gram said.

"Is she retired like you?" Ruth Rose asked.

"No, she's a docent," her gram said.

"What's a docent?" Josh asked.

"A docent is a guide who takes people through a museum," Gram Hathaway said. "Maria's specialty is silver and gold. She loves looking at all the priceless old things."

"I can't wait to meet her," Ruth Rose said.

"You'll love Maria," Gram said. "She likes to bake cookies."

"I like her already!" Josh said.

"But first we're going to Kip's Place," Gram said.

"Who's Kip, Gram?" Ruth Rose asked.

"He's a friend of Maria's, and he runs a very cool studio where artists can paint or sculpt or make stained-glass things," Gram explained. "Yesterday I made a clay vase on Kip's pottery wheel. He showed me a picture of an old vase, and I copied it. I must say, it turned out very nicely."

"Awesome, Gram," Ruth Rose said.

"I put it in Kip's kiln to dry overnight, so today it should be ready to decorate," Gram told them.

Dink, Josh, and Ruth Rose watched out the windows as their driver took them through heavy traffic. They saw thousands of cars and millions of people. The buildings were so tall that the kids couldn't see the sky.

Dink closed his eyes. After a few minutes, he moaned, "Oh no!"

"What's wrong?" Josh asked him.

"I'm under the ocean in a submarine," Dink whispered. "It's made of chocolate cake. I'm eating every bit. . . ."

Josh poked him. "You're cute, Newt," he said.

Soon the buildings they passed were shorter, and they could see the sky above them. There were fewer people on the sidewalks and less traffic on the streets.

"Are we in Brooklyn?" Dink asked the driver.

"Yes, sir," the man said. "Park Slope coming up! Got an address for me?"

"Take us to the corner of Twenty-Fifth Street and Fifth Avenue, please," Gram told him. A few minutes later, the driver pulled up to a row of storefronts. KIP'S PLACE was painted on a large window between a dry cleaner's and a sandwich shop called Wrap It Up.

"We're here!" Gram said, and they all got out of the taxi.

While Gram paid the driver, the kids walked to Kip's Place and peered through the window. They saw stacks of canvases waiting to be painted. A pottery wheel stood in a corner, near a kiln. Art supplies filled shelves against one wall.

"Let's go inside," Gram said.

Josh's leg brushed an old, crumbling gravestone that was leaning against the building. It was made of granite and stood about two feet tall. There were letters and numbers carved into the stone, but they were difficult to read. "Yuck," Josh muttered.

Just then, a thin guy came out the door. "See you later, Kip," he said, and walked down the street.

A tall man wearing a black apron over jeans stepped into the doorway. "Hi, Ms. Hathaway," he said to Gram.

"Hello, Kip," she said. "I brought my granddaughter and her friends. Kids, say hi to Kip Skane."

Kip wore purple-tinted sunglasses. His blond hair was in a ponytail. The kids introduced themselves and shook hands.

Kip's Place was one big room. Dink smelled paint and something sweet, like the glue he used to make models. Quiet music came from a speaker. In the back were two doors. One had a sign that said RESTROOM, and the other said PRIVATE. Between the doors were shelves that held jars of paint, pads of paper, paintbrushes, and a row of cans lined up like soldiers.

"Why do you have a gravestone outside?" Josh asked Kip.

"My cousin Bertie found that," Kip told Josh. "Some of my customers are into doing gravestone rubbings. I'll show you how, if you want."

"That's okay," Josh said. "I don't mess with gravestones!"

"Can you open the kiln?" Gram asked. "I can't wait to see how my vase turned out!"

"I put a couple more pieces in with your vase," Kip said. "Let's see what we have." He pulled a key from a pocket and inserted it into a lock on the kiln's door. He twisted a handle, and the door opened.

Everyone looked into the kiln. They saw a pile of broken clay pieces.

"What happened?" Gram cried. "My vase is smashed!"

"I'm so sorry, Ms. Hathaway!" Kip said. "This has never happened before. I must have set the heat too high."

Gram just shook her head. "The vase was a gift for Maria," she said. "I suppose I can make her another one."

"Of course you can!" Kip said. "In fact, you can start right now."

Gram looked at her watch. "No, it's almost noon," she said. "I want to get these kids settled, and I'll bet they're hungry enough to eat a horse!"

"Yes!" they all said at once.

"Or a spaceship," Dink whispered to Josh.

They left while Kip was pulling chunks of broken clay from the kiln.

"I'm sorry your vase got busted up," Dink said.

"Thanks, sweetie," Gram said. "I'll start another one tomorrow."

"Where does your friend live?" Ruth Rose asked her grandmother.

"Right around the corner on Twenty-Fifth Street," she answered.

A few minutes later, they stopped at a tall apartment building. A tree in front grew out of a small patch of grass. Daffodils around the tree's trunk waved their yellow heads in the breeze.

"Maria's on the fifth floor," Gram said. "But there's an elevator."

They entered the building and took the elevator. "Turn to the left," Gram said when they emerged from the car.

A short woman with red hair piled on

top of her head was standing a few feet away. Two men and a woman were with her, their backs to the elevator.

"Maria, this is my grand—" Gram started to say.

"Thank goodness you're here!" the small woman called. "I was so worried. These police officers are looking for you!"

CHAPTER 3

One of the men and the woman wore blue police uniforms. The second man was short and dressed in a dark suit and tie. He had a thin black mustache, and he kept blinking. His cheeks were shiny and pink, as if he'd just shaved. The man was holding something wrapped in newspaper.

"I don't understand, Maria," Gram said. "Police to see me?"

"Maybe we could all go inside," the female police officer suggested. She was tall and strong-looking. Her name tag read DEMING.

"Good idea," Maria said, opening her door wide.

They all walked into her living room. Two sofas faced each other in front of a fireplace. Dink saw hundreds of books on the shelves. A small table held a vase of daffodils. Empty vases stood in a row on the mantel over the fireplace. A cabinet held more vases behind a glass door.

"Kids, this is my best friend, Maria Hoffman," Gram said quietly to Dink, Josh, and Ruth Rose.

The kids said hi, but they couldn't take their eyes off the police officers.

The adults sat on the sofas. Gram and Maria sat next to one another, facing the officers and the man with the mustache. The kids plopped together on the floor.

The male officer said, "I'm Officer Pete Foster. That's Officer Tara Deming. This gentleman is Mr. Foley Royce. He asked us to come and chat with you, Ms. Hathaway."

"Chat about what?" Ruth Rose's gram asked.

"About this," Mr. Royce said, unwrapping the newspaper and revealing a tall vase. It seemed to be painted silver, and the silver was tarnished nearly black in some places. He set the vase on the coffee table.

"Ms. Hathaway, have you ever seen that vase?" asked Officer Deming.

"It looks like the vase I made yesterday," Gram said. "In Kip's Place, around the corner. But it can't be! Mine was broken in the kiln."

Gram leaned over and placed her hands on the vase. "I think it *is* mine," she said. "The clay is still a little soft." She reached a hand into the vase. "I put a note inside . . . but it's not here."

Officer Foster pulled a plastic baggie from a pocket and handed it to Gram. The baggie held a slip of paper. "Is this the note?" he asked. "Mr. Royce found it in the vase."

Gram held the baggie so she could see the paper. "It says my name and this address," she said. "I put it in my vase so it wouldn't get mixed up with some others. I don't understand this at all."

"Well, I understand!" Mr. Royce said. His voice was squeaky, like a little kid's. He had an accent, reminding Dink of the people he had met in London, England. "This is a cheap forgery of the Royce Vase!"

Gram shook her head. "I'm sorry, what is the Royce Vase?" she asked Foley Royce.

"In the 1800s, one of my ancestors bought a tall vase from a relative of Paul Revere, the famous silversmith," Mr. Royce said. "It is known as the Royce Vase. It's solid silver, extremely valuable, and was passed down in the family for generations!"

Everyone was staring at him.

"Please continue, Mr. Royce," said Officer Foster.

"My grandfather left instructions to have the Royce Vase interred with him in the family vault when he passed away. He hired a sculptor to carve a marble pedestal to hold the vase. Recently, I entered the Royce family crypt, in Green-Wood Cemetery. I knew immediately that the vase on the pedestal was a fake!"

Mr. Royce pointed to the vase in front of him, then glared at Gram. "You cleverly painted your clay vase so it would resemble silver, at least in a dark crypt," he said.

"I did no such thing!" Gram said. "I've never been to that cemetery!"

"Then please explain how your vase came to be on Grandfather's pedestal," Mr. Royce said. "And why the real Royce Vase is gone."

"I . . . I have no idea," Gram whispered. Maria took her hand and held it.

Dink, Josh, and Ruth Rose sat with their mouths open.

"The last time I saw this vase was when I made it," Gram went on. "Kip Skane will tell you the same thing."

"Nonsense," Mr. Royce said. His cheeks had turned even pinker.

"I'll talk to Mr. Skane," Officer Deming said. She wrote something in a small notebook.

"Ms. Hathaway, will you come to the police station with me?" Officer Foster asked.

"But why?" Gram asked.

"For your fingerprints," Officer Deming said. "You'll also need to give us a statement, which we'll type up and have you sign. Our detectives will want to ask more questions."

Gram stood up. "Of course I'll go with you," she said. "The sooner we clear this up, the better!"

"And you can tell these officers what you did with the Royce Vase!" Mr. Royce added. "You can keep your fake!"

He nodded to the officers and left the apartment.

Both officers stood up. Officer Foster rewrapped the clay vase and tucked it under his arm. "We'll take this for evidence," he said. "Are you ready to go, Ms. Hathaway?"

CHAPTER 4

Ruth Rose jumped up and stood next to her grandmother on the sofa. "What's going to happen?" she asked. "Are you going to jail?"

"We have to question your grandmother," Officer Foster explained. "She's not under arrest."

"I'm fine," Gram said. "You kids stay with Maria. We'll get this straightened out, and I'll be back before you know it!"

Gram stood up, giving Ruth Rose a hug. "I'm ready," she told the two officers.

When Officers Deming and Foster

escorted Gram from the apartment, the kids had tears in their eyes. Maria put her arms around them. "No crying allowed!" she said. "How about a yummy snack? And while you're eating, I'll see if I can find my attorney on a Sunday afternoon!"

She brought out apple slices, chocolate chip cookies, and milk. The kids sat back on the sofa, and Maria went into her bedroom.

"This whole thing stinks!" Ruth Rose said.

"No way!" Josh said. "I love cookies."

"She's not talking about food, Josh," Dink said.

"Guys, if that really was Gram's vase, it didn't get broken in the kiln last night," Ruth Rose said. "But I don't understand how it got from Kip's studio to some cemetery!"

"If Mr. Royce is right, *someone* brought it there. They took the real Royce Vase off the pedestal and left your gram's vase," Dink said.

"Okay, I get that," Ruth Rose said. "But whoever made the switch had to know about Gram's vase. Who could that be?"

Josh sipped his milk. "Anyone in Kip's Place could have seen the vase your grandmother made," he said. "People who went there to do art stuff."

Ruth Rose shoved her plate aside. "Okay, other people probably knew about Gram's vase," she said. "But how would someone know there was a silver vase that looked just like Gram's in that crypt?"

"Mr. Royce knew," Josh said. "Maybe *he* took the vase, and he's trying to blame your grandmother."

"But how would Mr. Royce know about my grandmother's vase in Kip's Place?" Ruth Rose asked. "It doesn't make sense."

"Also, why would Mr. Royce want to steal a vase that was already in his family?" Dink asked. "You're right, Ruth Rose—it doesn't make sense."

Dink put the milk carton in the fridge. Ruth Rose carried her plate and glass to the sink. "Let's go!" she said.

Josh swiped a final cookie from the plate. "Where?" he asked.

"Right now, all we have are questions," Ruth Rose said, grabbing her backpack. "I want some answers!" She walked over to Maria's bedroom door and knocked.

The door opened, and Maria stood there with her cell phone clamped to one ear. She held up one finger to Ruth Rose, then rolled her eyes and tossed her phone onto the bed. "Lawyers!" she said. "What can I do for you, sweetie? Need more food?"

"We want to go . . . exploring," Ruth Rose said.

"Exploring?" Maria said.

"We just want to check out the neighborhood," Ruth Rose said. "Dink has a cell phone, so you two can exchange numbers."

"I guess that'll be okay, then," Maria said, reaching for her phone. "It's one-thirty. Please be back in an hour."

"We will," Ruth Rose said.

Dink pulled his phone from his back pocket, and they tapped each other's numbers into their contacts.

"Watch when you cross streets," Maria said. "And call me if you get lost!"

"We will," Dink said. "And thanks for everything."

"You're welcome," Maria said. She was already texting on her phone.

The kids left the apartment and walked to the elevator.

"What are we exploring?" Josh asked. "You heard Maria—we could get lost in Brooklyn!"

"No one's getting lost," Ruth Rose

said. "We're going to Kip's Place to find out how Gram's vase got stolen."

The elevator took them down, and they walked out to the street.

"What time does it get dark in October in Brooklyn?" Josh asked, looking at the sky.

"Don't worry," Ruth Rose said. "We'll be back before supper."

"I'm not worried about supper," Josh said.

Dink poked him. "Oh yeah?"

Josh laughed. "Okay, I am worried about supper."

They walked to a light at a corner and crossed Twenty-Fifth Street to Fifth Avenue. Five minutes later, they were looking at Kip through his window. He was standing with a woman at a worktable and showing her how to cut pieces of colored glass.

At another table, a man was sketching on a large pad.

Kip looked up when the kids walked in. "We were wrong about your grandmother's vase," he said, peering at Ruth Rose through his purple sunglasses. "It didn't get destroyed in my kiln. Actually, I forgot to turn the kiln on before I went to bed. So I got up in the middle of the night and turned it on. I was so sleepy, I must have set the temperature too high, and another piece of pottery broke. But I think someone stole your grandmother's vase out of the kiln last night, before I turned it on!"

"I know. We just saw the vase!" Ruth Rose said. She told Kip about Mr. Royce and how he'd found Gram's vase in his family crypt. "And a silver vase that was *supposed* to be in the crypt was missing. Somebody switched them!"

"They took her grandmother to the police station!" Josh added.

Kip stared at the kids. "That's horrible!" he said. "Give me a minute to finish up with Dawn. Then I want to show you something."

While they waited, Dink looked at clay art displayed on a shelf. There was a mug, a small bowl, two vases, and what looked like a cat. Tacked to the edge of the shelf were photos of a mug, a bowl, a vase on a table, and a cat. Dink figured Kip put these pictures there so people would have something to copy for their projects.

Kip motioned for the kids to follow him. He opened a door labeled RESTROOM and took the kids down a short hallway. At the end was another door that led outside. Next to it was a bathroom. That door was open, and Kip pointed inside. "Take a look at that," he said.

There was a window over the toilet, but the glass was broken. Cool air blew inside. A few jagged pieces of glass stuck out of the window frame, reminding Dink of sharks' teeth. The rest of the glass was scattered over the bathroom floor.

CHAPTER 5

"This is how the thief got in," Kip said. He pointed to a rock on the floor. "He must have used that to smash the glass."

"Oh my gosh!" Ruth Rose said. "Did you call the police?"

"Officer Deming was here just a few minutes ago," Kip said. "She asked me if your grandmother's vase got destroyed in my kiln. I told her I thought so at first. But then I found this broken window and realized the vase got stolen from the kiln!"

They walked back to the art room. "Did the thief take anything else?" Dink asked.

Kip hesitated. "Yeah, he took a few dollars from my desk," he said. "And a stained-glass panel is missing."

"Then that explains how Gram's vase got inside the crypt," Ruth Rose said. "The crook took it there to switch for the valuable one!"

Just then, a man in gray coveralls came through the front door. "You Mr. Skane?" he asked Kip. "I'm Gus, come to fix your window."

"Great," Kip said. "Come on—I'll show you."

The kids left Kip's Place and headed for Twenty-Fifth Street.

A small sign on a post near the traffic light said GREEN-WOOD CEMETERY, with an arrow.

"That's where the crypt is," Dink said. He gave Ruth Rose a look.

She nodded. "Let's go see this crypt where Mr. Royce says my grandmother stole his famous vase!" she said.

"I'm good here, guys," Josh said. "You go ahead."

"Come on," Ruth Rose said. "Don't you want to help my grandmother?"

Josh shook his head.

"You don't want to help her?" Dink said.

"I *do* want to help her," Josh said. "I just don't want to go to a cemetery to do it!"

"But that's the scene of the crime!" Ruth Rose said.

"Yeah, I know, but . . . ," Josh started to say.

The light changed to WALK. Ruth Rose and Dink linked arms with Josh and marched him across the street.

"I have a bad feeling about this," Josh said. He started tugging another loose strand of sweater yarn, then stopped and jammed his hands into his pockets.

"Well, I have a good feeling about it," Rose said. "Plus, I'm not going to sit

around and do nothing while my grandmother is in trouble!"

On the other side of the street, Dink
saw a broken bottle on the ground. He
stared at the bottle, thinking about Kip's
bathroom window. Broken pieces of glass
had been scattered on the floor. Sharp,
jagged glass had stuck out of the window's wooden frame.

A thought slithered through Dink's
mind, like a fast-moving snake. Then the
thought was gone.

"Hey, Earth to Dink," Josh said, nudging his friend.

"Sorry," Dink said. "Just thinking
about something."

They saw the entrance to the cemetery in the distance. It was a massive
stone structure with two archways, like
a cathedral built hundreds of years ago.
Stone buildings stood on each side of the
entry, with flowers planted in front.

"Guys, listen!" Josh said, pointing up.

Bird chirps echoed down from the ceiling of the entryway.

Dink noticed a brass sign fastened to one of the stones. He read it to Josh and Ruth Rose:

ENJOY THE BEAUTIFUL AND
CHATTY MONK PARAKEETS THAT
LIVE IN GREEN-WOOD CEMETERY.
ARGENTINA IS THEIR HOME, BUT
SOME ESCAPED IN THE 1960S
WHILE BEING BROUGHT TO PET
SHOPS IN AMERICA. THE PARAKEETS
ARE FRIENDLY, BUT PLEASE
DO NOT FEED THEM!

The kids looked up and saw dozens of green parakeets peering out from among the stones. They flew around the archway, making loud noises.

"I wonder what they're saying," Josh said.

Dink put his arm around Josh's shoulder. "They're saying 'Josh is going into a *cemetery*!'"

"Yeah, but I'm being *forced* to go there by my two best friends!" Josh said. They walked through the entryway, with parakeets flying over their heads.

Ruth Rose noticed a sign on one of the buildings that said OFFICE—FREE MAPS, and the kids went in.

Inside, Ruth Rose took a map from a rack near the door. She unfolded it, revealing what looked like miles of roads and pathways winding through the cemetery. Rows of gravestones stood on lawns around ponds and flower gardens.

"This says there are 560,000 graves here!" she said. "How will we find the Royce crypt?"

"Easy peasy," Dink said. "We ask."

A young guy was standing behind a counter, typing on a laptop. He wore a green shirt with GREEN-WOOD CEMETERY stitched on one sleeve. A white name tag that said PACO was pinned to the pocket.

"Hi," Dink said. "Can you tell us where the Royce crypt is?"

"Sure can," Paco said. "Got a map?"

Ruth Rose held up the map.

"Okay, hold on a second." Paco hit a

few keys on his laptop, then held out a hand. "Map, please."

Ruth Rose handed it over the counter. Paco checked his computer screen, then drew a circle on the map and handed it back to Ruth Rose. "It's near the edge of this pond," he said, tapping a blue area near his circle. "Outside, go right and walk a few hundred yards. The pond will be on the right, with a bunch of tiny buildings on the left. Those are the vaults, or crypts. Look for a door with a sign that says the name of the interred."

The kids thanked Paco and walked outside. They followed his directions, passing dozens of white gravestones set into the grass.

"What's *interred*?" Josh asked.

"I think it means buried," Dink answered.

"That's what I was afraid you'd say," Josh muttered.

CHAPTER 6

Two minutes later, they came to the pond. A few ducks were pecking at tall weeds that grew out of the water. A man in work clothes and boots was mowing the grass along the bank. When he noticed the kids, he stopped mowing and watched them. He walked over, wiping a sleeve across his face.

"Can I help you?" the man asked. His face and hands were tanned. The name ALBERT was sewn into the pocket of his shirt.

"We're looking for the Royce crypt," Dink said.

Albert raised his eyebrows and stared at Dink without blinking. His eyes were light brown. "What for?" he asked.

"Um, it's for my grandmother," Ruth Rose said. "She's an artist, and she loves old . . . things. I want to take a picture for her."

Albert nodded and pointed a finger. "Third vault on the right," he said.

They thanked him, then walked away. Dink had a feeling the man was watching them, and turned around quickly. He was right. The guy *was* staring after them, and Dink felt the skin on his arms get goose bumpy.

The kids came to a row of small stone buildings. They looked alike. Most had steps leading down to a padlocked door. There were no windows. Next to the locked door handles were brass plaques.

A minute later, they stood in front of the Royce vault. Dink pointed to the plaque attached to the stone wall with iron brackets. ROYCE, BUILT 1890 was written in raised letters. Dink looked over his shoulder, but the lawn mower guy was nowhere in sight.

The building's stone sides and steps were covered with furry green moss. A tree towered over the little building, blocking out the sun. A thick vine had grown up the tree trunk. Shiny ivy leaves had spread over the crypt's roof and covered its sides.

Dink gulped. The hair on his arms stood up. He was reminded of a witch's hut from a scary book his dad had read him when he was little.

"There's no padlock like on the other crypts," Ruth Rose said. "But there's a plastic tie to keep the door closed."

"I'll bet the police took the lock to check for your grandmother's fingerprints," Dink said.

"I can cut the plastic with my knife." Ruth Rose dug in her backpack and pulled out a red Swiss Army knife. "It matches my outfit!" she said.

"Whoa," Josh said. "These crypts are locked because people aren't supposed to go in!"

"There isn't a Do Not Enter sign," Ruth Rose said. "Besides, we'll only stay a minute, and we won't touch anything. Right, guys?"

"Right," Dink said.

"I'm keeping my hands in my pockets," Josh said.

Just then, a green blur flew out of the tree over their heads. A parakeet with a stick in its mouth landed on the plaque.

The bird looked at the kids through tiny black eyes. Two seconds later, it dropped the stick, flew up the side of the building, and disappeared through an opening in the vine leaves.

"Guys, it went inside the crypt!" Josh said. "There's a hole!"

"If birds can go in, so can we!" Ruth Rose went down the steps, cut the plastic tie, and pushed on the door. It stayed shut, so she tried pulling. This time, the door opened.

The parakeet zoomed back out, nearly colliding with Dink's shoulder. It landed on a tree branch over their heads. Ruth Rose pulled the door open wider, making the hinges squeak.

"I am so not going in there," Josh announced. "Dink, let me have your phone so I can call a cab."

"Joshua Pinto!" Ruth Rose said. "We are your best friends, and we are not going to leave you out here all alone with

560,000 dead people! Come in with us, please."

Josh took a baby step. "Okay, but if I see one dead body, I'll be up in that tree with Mr. Parakeet!" he said.

Ruth Rose pulled the door open all the way.

"Wait a sec," Dink said, taking his cell phone from a pocket. "I want a picture of you guys going into a crypt!" He took the picture and checked the result.

Dink and Josh followed Ruth Rose

down the steps. Josh made sure the door was left partly open.

They tiptoed into a dark room about the size of Dink's bedroom. Light from the doorway showed a floor and walls made of stone. Dink could feel the cold dampness through his clothing. The place smelled like a blanket that had been left out in the rain.

The corners were dark. The ceiling was low. Dink wiped a cobweb from his face. He snapped a picture of a pedestal near a wall. There was nothing else in the room except a pile of dead flower stalks on the floor. They were tied together with a rotting white ribbon.

"Yuck," Josh said, kicking at them. "Oh, double yuck!" One of the brown stalks turned out to be the skeleton of a bird that had been dead for a long time. A few feathers still clung to the sad little corpse.

"There's your dead body," Dink said,

grinning at Josh. "Are you going to fly away, Mr. Parakeet?"

"I meant a human body," Josh said. "Can we leave now? This isn't fun."

"We didn't come here to have fun," Ruth Rose said. "And I don't think my grandmother broke in here and stole a vase, either."

A small circle of light came from the front wall. It shone on one corner of the floor, like the beam from a flashlight.

"What's that light from?" Josh asked.

Dink pointed up at the wall. "It's the sun coming through that hole where the parakeet flew in," he said.

"But what's the hole for?" Josh insisted.

"It could be an air vent," Ruth Rose said.

"Dead guys don't need air," Josh muttered.

"It's not an air vent," Dink whispered. "The hole is so Royce ghosts can fly in and out."

"It's a shame your jokes are lame," Josh said. "And it's creepy in here!"

Dink turned on the flashlight on his phone. He shone the light around the room. "Because you're my friend," he told Josh.

"Thank you," Josh said. "But I'm still creeped."

"Well, don't get used to it, because my phone's running out of power," Dink mumbled as he lit up the pedestal.

It was made of smooth white marble and stood about three feet tall. The letter *R* had been carved into the base. The pedestal and the floor around it were dusty.

"Guys, look at this," Ruth Rose said. She pointed to a circle on top of the pedestal that was dust-free. "I'll bet this is where the Royce Vase was."

Behind the pedestal, a tattered velvet drape hung on the wall. It looked and smelled a hundred years old. The letter

R was sewn onto the center of the drape. There were holes and rips in the cloth, as if something had been chewing on it.

"The *R* must stand for *Royce,*" Josh said. "Like the one on the pedestal."

"I wonder where old Mr. Royce's body is," Ruth Rose said.

Dink swung his light around. It lit up some words on a brass plate embedded in the stone floor. He knelt down and wiped away dust and dirt. Then he read out loud:

JOSEPH ROYCE, 1822–1890.
MAY HE REST IN PEACE.

"He's under this *floor*?" Josh whispered.
"I guess so," Dink said.

CHAPTER 7

Josh backed away. "Guys, I'm going to have nightmares for the rest of my life," he said. "Can we please—"

Just then, the light from Dink's phone went out.

"What happened?" Josh cried.

"Sorry," Dink said. "My phone's dead."

"Perfect," Josh said. "We've got dead birds and dead batteries."

"Don't worry," Ruth Rose said. She was digging around in her backpack. "Aha!" She brought out a small flashlight and turned it on.

"Please tell me *your* batteries are

working," Josh said.

"Of course they are," Ruth Rose said. "We have plenty of light!"

Dink heard a noise behind him. He turned just as the door slammed shut.

"Okay, Dink," Josh said. "Thanks for trying to scare me to death!"

"I didn't shut the door," Dink said.

"Maybe it was the wind," Ruth Rose said. She aimed her flashlight at the door. It was definitely closed.

"Stop fooling around," Josh said, sprinting for the door. "Help me, okay?"

The three kids leaned against the door and pushed. It didn't move an inch.

"It's locked on the outside," Ruth Rose said.

"So this isn't a joke?" Josh asked. "We *are* locked in here?"

"Yes, but don't worry," Ruth Rose said. "Dink can call someone."

"My phone battery's dead, remember?" Dink said.

The three kids stared at each other over the beam from Ruth Rose's flashlight.

"So we have light, but we'll starve to death," Josh said.

"No, we won't," Ruth Rose said. She handed Josh her flashlight and opened her backpack. She pulled out a package of peanut butter crackers.

Dink moved to the far corner and sat next to the round beam of light from the parakeet's hole.

"Josh, I think you should shut off my flashlight," Ruth Rose said. "We're wasting the batteries. Our eyes will adjust to the dark in a few minutes."

"Great," Josh mumbled, but he switched off the flashlight.

"Ouch!" Dink cried. A tiny drop of blood appeared on his finger.

"What's wrong?" Ruth Rose asked.

"Something on the floor cut my finger," Dink said.

Ruth Rose walked to where Dink was

sitting. She crouched down and looked at the round spot where the light from the hole lit up the floor. "There are tiny pieces of glass," she said. She gathered them into a tissue.

"Can I have one of those tissues?" Dink asked. She handed him one, and he wrapped it around his finger.

"Josh, do you want a cracker?" Ruth Rose asked.

"No, I want a stick of dynamite to blow this door open," he answered. Then he walked over and sat between Dink and Ruth Rose. "But I'll take a cracker."

They each ate a cracker.

"A hundred years from now, someone will find my skeleton, like that bird's," Josh said. He began pulling on the strand of yarn hanging from his sweater sleeve. "They'll name this place the Joshua Pinto Crypt."

"We have plenty of oxygen," Ruth Rose said. She pointed at the hole. "We just need to figure out how to get out of here."

"Maybe I can squeeze through that hole," Josh said.

"Josh, it's only six inches across," Dink said. "And it's eight feet off the floor."

Josh walked over and stood under the hole. He shouted, "HELP! WE'RE LOCKED IN! HELP!"

"Josh, these walls are about a foot thick," Ruth Rose said. "Solid stone."

"But if we all yell, someone might

hear us," Josh said, pointing up. "Through that parakeet hole!"

"It's worth a try," Dink said. He and Ruth Rose stood next to Josh and yelled, "HELP! WE NEED HELP! HELLLLP!" They continued yelling until their throats got sore.

Dink put his ear against the door. "Nothing," he said. He sat on the floor with his back against the pedestal. Josh and Ruth Rose sat next to him.

"Why couldn't I be Gummy Guy?" Josh muttered.

"Who's that?" Ruth Rose asked.

"He's a guy in my comics," Josh said. "He can stretch himself real thin like a rubber band, only he's made of candy. He could slip through that hole like a snake!"

"I might have some candy," Ruth Rose said. She felt around inside her backpack. "Sorry."

"No candy, Andy," Dink joked, but he felt like crying.

Ruth Rose pulled her scarf from her backpack and started to wrap it around her neck. "I have an idea!" she cried. "Josh, pull a piece of yarn from your sweater!"

"Why? You always tell me not to," he said, but started tugging on the yarn.

"What's your idea?" Dink asked Ruth Rose.

"If we tie Josh's yarn to my scarf, we can dangle it outside that hole," she said. "The scarf is bright red. Somebody is bound to see it!"

Dink got up. "That could work," he said. "But how do we get the scarf through the hole? It's too high for us to reach."

"We need Gummy Guy," Josh said. "He could reach it!"

"We need a ladder," Dink said.

"Guys, we can use this!" Ruth Rose said. She turned and put her hands on the pedestal. "If we drag this under the hole, Josh can climb on it because he's tallest. Then he can poke the scarf through the hole!"

They grabbed the pedestal and tried to move it.

"Stupid thing won't budge," Josh said.

"It's solid marble," Dink said. "And

probably weighs more than the three of us together."

"Got another idea," Josh said. He tugged on the velvet drape. The rotted fabric fell to the floor, leaving a long curtain rod. Josh stood on the pedestal and lifted the rod out of the wall brackets that held it in place.

"What are you going to use that for?" Dink asked.

"We can tie the scarf to one end of the pole," Josh said. "I think the pole is long enough to reach through the hole!"

"Now I get it!" Dink said. "Pretty smart, Art!"

"You're right, Dwight," Josh said.

Josh held the curtain rod while Dink tied the scarf to one end.

"Tie it tight," Ruth Rose said. "I don't want to lose my favorite scarf!"

Dink gave the knot an extra tug. Josh held the curtain rod up against the wall until the scarf was in front of the parakeet's hole. After some poking, he was finally able to force the scarf through the hole.

"Now let's just hope someone sees it," Ruth Rose said.

Dink checked his watch. The numbers glowed in the dark. "Maria is expecting us home in ten minutes!" he said.

CHAPTER 8

Nothing happened.

"Let me try," Dink said. He took the pole from Josh and jiggled it up and down. He pretended he was fishing and the bright red scarf was the worm on his line.

A few minutes later, they heard a knock on the door. "Yo, is anybody in there?" a voice yelled.

"YES!" the kids all cried together. "WE'RE LOCKED IN!"

"Okay, wait a minute!" the voice outside said.

And then the door opened, letting in fresh air and sunshine.

A man in a T-shirt and running shorts was standing there. He was surprised to see the three kids rush out of the crypt.

"How the heck did you get in there?" the man asked.

"We were exploring the crypt, and we got locked in," Ruth Rose said. She untied her scarf and put it around her neck.

"How did the door get locked?" Dink asked.

The man showed the kids a stick he was holding. "This was jammed inside that metal hasp loop," he said. "No matter how hard you pushed, it wouldn't budge. Good thing I saw your red flag!"

"Yeah, good thing," Josh said. "All we had to eat was one lousy cracker!"

"Bummer," the man said. "Have a nice day!" He jogged down the path.

"Thank you!" the kids called after him.

"How do you think a stick got through that loop thing?" Ruth Rose asked.

"I'll bet the parakeet did it," Josh said. "Maybe he thinks this crypt is his private place."

Dink shook his head as he looked at his watch. "Guys, it's after two-thirty!" he said. "We're supposed to be back at Maria's place!"

It took the kids ten minutes to get back to the apartment. They rode the elevator to the fifth floor, where they found a note taped to Maria's door:

> *Where were you???*
> *I tried to text Dink. No luck.*
> *I'm at the police station.*
> *Heading to Kip's Place.*
> *Meet me there.*
>
> —*M.H.*

"She didn't say anything about Gram," Ruth Rose said.

"Maria told us she's getting a lawyer," Dink reminded her. "Maybe she'll have good news when we see her."

They left the building and headed for Kip's. "All this exploring is making me hungry," Josh said. "That cracker in my stomach is very lonely!"

"I have some money," Dink said. "I'll treat us to lunch at that sandwich place."

When they got to the traffic light across from Kip's Place, they saw a white van parked in the alley between Kip's Place and Wrap It Up. A sign on the van's door said GUS'S GLASS REPAIR.

The light turned to WALK, and the kids crossed to Kip's Place and went in. The second door in the rear wall was open, revealing a small office. Kip was sitting at a desk in front of a laptop.

"Maria isn't here," Ruth Rose said.

Dink looked at the floor under his feet. He saw tiny pieces of colored glass.

Kip noticed the kids. "Be out in a minute," he said.

While they waited, Dink glanced at

the pictures tacked to the shelf above the pottery wheel. He stepped closer to the photo of the vase, and he saw numbers and letters on the picture: *21H—7W.*

Kip came out of his office and closed the door. "What's going on?" he asked.

"We went to see—" Josh started.

"To see Ruth Rose's grandmother," Dink interrupted. "She's still at the police station, but they let us talk to her. We even had lunch with her, right, guys? Those sandwiches were awesome!"

Ruth Rose and Josh stared at Dink.

"Um, okay, we'll just take off," Dink said. "Just wanted to say . . . hi."

"Where are you headed?" Kip asked.

"Um . . . ," Dink said.

"Dink's buying us lunch!" Josh said.

"I thought you had lunch with Ms. Hathaway," Kip said. "At the police station." He stared at them through his purple sunglasses.

Dink let out a laugh. "Josh likes two lunches," he said.

Just then, a woman walked into Kip's Place. The kids had seen her earlier. She waved to Kip and hung her jacket over a chair. The woman opened a drawer under a worktable and pulled out sheets of colored glass.

"Be right with you, Dawn," Kip told her. He walked to the door and opened it for the kids. "Have a nice second lunch."

Dink watched the woman begin to cut a piece of yellow glass with a small metal tool.

"If my grandmother's friend comes, will you please tell her we're having lunch next door?" Ruth Rose asked. "Her name is Maria, and she has red hair."

"I know Maria," Kip said. "She's one of my favorite customers."

CHAPTER 9

Inside the sandwich shop, the kids chose a booth next to a window. A server brought them shiny plastic menus. "My name is Simon," he told them. "What'll you have?"

They each ordered a shrimp wrap and lemonade. Simon came back with straws and napkins.

"Do you have a charger cord I can borrow?" Dink asked. "I need to charge my phone."

"I can lend you mine," Simon said. "Be right back."

Josh ripped the end off his straw

wrapper and blew the paper tube at Dink. *"Awesome sandwiches?"* he said. "You told Kip a big, fat lie!"

"I didn't know what else to say," Dink admitted. "I didn't want Kip to know we'd been to the cemetery."

Simon brought a cord and plugged it into an outlet. "See if this works," he told Dink.

Dink inserted the cord's other end into his phone. "It's perfect, thank you!" he said. Simon gave him a thumbs-up and walked away.

"Why didn't you want Kip to know we went to the crypt?" Ruth Rose asked.

"Because I think something weird is going on in his studio," Dink said in a low voice. He glanced through the window at a sign painted on the side of the repair van. It said LET GUS FIX THIS! below a drawing of a window frame with most of the glass missing and sharp pieces sticking out of it.

"Funny weird or scary weird?" Josh asked Dink.

Dink pointed at the van. "See that sign?" he asked. "Well, if you were a robber, would you crawl through a window with sharp pieces of glass sticking out of the frame?"

"I wouldn't," Ruth Rose said.

"Me either," Dink said. "You'd break out all the sharp pieces, right? But the broken window in Kip's bathroom still had those jagged pieces."

"So what's the weird part?" Josh asked.

Dink thought for a minute. "Guys, I don't think any burglar climbed through that window," he said. "They'd get cut."

"But why smash the window and not climb through it?" Josh asked.

"I don't know," Dink said. *"That's* weird, right?"

"But *somebody* stole Gram's vase from Kip's Place," Ruth Rose said. "How did the robber get in?"

"I don't know that, either," Dink said.

Simon came with their food, and they started eating. After a few minutes, Dink wiped his mouth and said, "Ruth Rose, do you still have the pieces of glass you picked up in the crypt? When I cut my finger?"

Ruth Rose unwrapped the tissue, revealing a bunch of glass slivers.

"They're all different colors," Josh said.

"Right," Dink said. "They're exactly like the pieces I just saw on Kip's floor. What if someone from Kip's Place had bits of glass on the bottom of his feet, and carried it into the crypt?"

"And *that* person stole the Royce Vase?" Ruth Rose asked.

Dink nodded. "Yes! They brought your gram's vase to make the switch, and they didn't realize they were also bring-ing pieces of glass and leaving them on the crypt floor."

"But who?" Josh asked.

Dink shrugged and sipped his drink. "Kip gets a lot of customers coming in there," he said. "Maybe one of them stole a key and returned later to get the vase from the kiln."

"Like that woman who came in," Ruth Rose said. "Dawn."

"She was making something out of stained glass!" Josh said.

Dink nodded. "Yeah, and she was wearing running shoes," he said. "Little pieces of glass could get stuck in those grooves on the bottom. My sneakers pick up stuff all the time."

"Don't forget *we* were walking around Kip's, too," Josh said. "Maybe the glass in the crypt came off *our* feet."

Dink shook his head. "I don't think it was one of us. When I cut my finger, I was sitting way back in that corner," he said. "None of us walked in that part of the crypt."

"Guys, that crypt must have had a big padlock on the door, like the others," Josh said. "So how did the vase thief get in?"

"Josh is right," Ruth Rose said. "Maybe someone did steal Kip's key to rob Gram's vase, but they'd have to steal *another* key to get into the crypt."

The kids thought about that. "I wonder where the cemetery keeps those keys," Dink said.

"I know who probably has a key to the Royce crypt," Josh said. "Foley Royce!"

"But he's from England, and he's never even heard of my grandmother or Kip," Ruth Rose said. "So how would *he* be able to swap the vases?"

The door banged open, and Maria rushed in, holding her cell phone. "There you are!" she exclaimed. "My poor feet! I practically ran over here! Good thing I wore running shoes!" She plunked her phone on the table and sat next to Ruth

Rose. She stretched out her legs, with her feet on the seat next to Dink.

When Dink slid over to make room, he noticed the bottoms of Maria's sneakers. Caught between the rubber ridges were slivers of blue, green, and red glass.

Dink looked away. When he reached for his lemonade, his hand shook.

Was Maria the person who snuck into the crypt?

Did *she* steal the Royce Vase?

CHAPTER 10

Simon came over, and Maria asked for a glass of water.

Dink stopped himself from staring at the soles of her sneakers. But he couldn't stop *thinking* about them. He snuck a peek at Maria. She didn't look like a thief. But what did thieves look like?

Dink couldn't finish his sandwich.

Think, Dink, he told himself.

Ruth Rose's grandmother had said Maria Hoffman liked valuable things.

Maria knew about the vase Gram Hathaway had made.

Because of her museum work, she

probably knew the Royce Vase was in the family crypt. And the cemetery was a short walk from her apartment!

Dink wiped his hands on his napkin. He tried to make sense of it all. At home, he wrote lists when he was confused, so he made a mental list now:

1. Maybe Maria knew the vase was in the crypt.
2. Maybe she also knew Ruth Rose's grandmother was a good pottery maker.
3. Maybe she downloaded a picture of the Royce Vase.
4. Maybe she asked Ruth Rose's grandmother to make her one like it.
5. Then maybe she got into Kip's Place and took the vase.
6. Next, she went to the crypt and made the switch.
7. It was all possible.

"Earth to Dink," Josh said, nudging him.

"Sorry," Dink said. All the maybes were giving him a headache.

"Did you see Gram?" Ruth Rose asked Maria.

"Yes. She's fine and sends her love, but I'm afraid that's the only good news," Maria said. "The police think they found evidence she was in that crypt, and they want to keep her there a little longer while they investigate."

"What kind of evidence?" Dink asked.

"Pieces of glass," Maria said. "They still think she swapped her vase for the Royce Vase. I told them that was absurd, but they're keeping her until—"

"She has to stay at the police station?" Ruth Rose interrupted.

"I'm afraid so, dear," Maria said. "But at least she's not in a jail cell. They have a little room. She has a TV and a tiny window."

She reached across the table and gave Ruth Rose's hand a squeeze. "Just until the police can find the real thief."

Or until we do, Dink thought.

"But," Maria went on, "my attorney, Lanny, has promised to call. So let's get you kids settled in. I have—"

Just then, Maria's phone rang. "That will be Lanny!" she said. She grabbed the phone and hurried outside.

Dink leaned over the table. "Guys, I think *she* stole the vase!" he hissed.

"Who, Lanny?" Josh said.

"No, *Maria!*"

Josh and Ruth Rose stared at Dink.

Maria sailed back in, slipping her phone into a pocket. "Lanny is meeting me and your dear grandmother at the police station in an hour with a plan," she said. "Let's go home."

Dink paid Simon, and the kids followed Maria out to the street. Gus's repair van was still parked in the alley.

When they walked behind the van, Dink saw a big black *G* painted across the rear doors. *G* stood for *Gus,* he guessed. And then he remembered something.

"Wait, I want to go into Kip's for a minute," Dink said.

"Why?" Josh asked.

Without answering, Dink zipped through Kip's front door. Dawn was cleaning her worktable. Kip was on the phone in his office and didn't notice Dink.

Dink whipped out his phone, took a picture, and was out the door in less than a minute.

While they walked toward Maria's apartment building, Dink was forming a plan.

Inside the apartment, Maria pulled three sleeping bags from a closet.

"Now I'm going to find a cab to go to the police station," she said. "If Lanny can work her magic, I'll bring Gram Hathaway back."

As soon as Maria was out the door, Ruth Rose grabbed Dink by the arm. "What do you mean, you think Maria is the crook?" she asked. "She and Gram have been best friends forever!"

"Maria has pieces of glass stuck in the bottom of her sneakers," Dink said. "And that's not all."

Dink grabbed a pillow off a sofa and sat on the floor. Josh and Ruth Rose did the same. "Here's what I think," he said. "Maria knows a lot about old gold and silver stuff, so she probably knows the Royce Vase is worth a lot of money. And she made a plan to get it. She also knew it was in the crypt. Your grandmother's vase gave her the idea to switch the two."

"But why did Maria need Gram's vase?" Ruth Rose asked. "Why didn't she just break into the crypt and take the Royce Vase?"

"Because of the dead guy's family," Dink said.

"The family?" Josh asked.

"The Royce relatives," Dink said. "Maria must know there are still some around. If a family member visited the crypt and the Royce Vase wasn't on that pedestal, they'd call the cops. And the cops would look for people who know a lot about old silver. Sooner or later, they'd check out the museum where Maria works. And Maria couldn't take that chance."

"So she had to put another vase in its place just in case," Josh said. He laughed. "Hey, I made a poem!"

Dink nodded. "We know Maria goes to Kip's a lot. She could have grabbed silver paint from his shelf when she stole your grandmother's vase," he said. "Then she painted the vase before she brought it to the crypt."

"So what do we do?" Ruth Rose asked.

"I'm not finished," Dink said.

CHAPTER 11

Dink took out his phone and found his recent photos. He showed Josh and Ruth Rose the one from when they arrived at the crypt.

"Josh looks scared," Ruth Rose said.

"Not scared," Josh said. "Just careful."

Dink swiped his phone screen to look at more pictures. "Look at that pedestal," Dink said. He was glad to see that the *R* on the pedestal's base was clearly shown. "There's the *R* for *Royce.*"

Dink swiped again, bringing up the picture he had just taken at Kip's. "*This* shows a picture tacked to one of Kip's shelves," he explained. "It's a photo of the Royce Vase, sitting on that same marble pedestal inside the crypt. I think Ruth Rose's gram was looking at this picture when she made her vase, which explains why hers looks like the Royce Vase."

They all stared at the picture.

"I think Maria had found that picture of the Royce Vase in one of her books, and your grandmother made *her* vase look just like it," he told Ruth Rose. "Only your grandmother didn't know anything about the Royce Vase. She was just copying Maria's picture."

"But how did *Kip* get the picture of the Royce Vase?" Ruth Rose asked.

"Maria probably texted it to him, and he printed it," Dink said. "Kip did tell us Maria was a good customer of his."

"I can't believe Maria would steal something and let Gram take the blame," Ruth Rose said.

Dink stood up. "Let's search this place while she's gone," he said.

"For what?" Josh asked.

"For the Royce Vase!"

"But she's got tons of vases," Ruth Rose said. "Gram said she collects them." She pointed to the bookshelves. "Look at all those, and there are probably more."

Dink held up his phone. "But we have my picture of Kip's picture of the Royce Vase, so we know what it looks like."

Josh took Dink's phone and made the image larger. "Hmm . . . *21H—7W*. I'll bet these letters and numbers tell how big the vase is," he said. "*H* must stand for *height,* so the vase is twenty-one inches high. *W* is for *width,* so it's seven inches wide."

"I think you're right," Dink said. "Let's start searching before Maria gets back. Look for silver paint, too."

"I'll take the bedroom," Ruth Rose said as she turned in that direction.

"I'll check out the kitchen," Josh said.

"Remember you're looking for a vase," Dink said. "Not cookies."

Josh laughed and headed for the kitchen.

Dink wandered around the living room. He found vases in cupboards. More stood on bookshelves, small tables, and even windowsills. There was a special cabinet with at least a dozen glass vases. He counted twenty-seven vases in the room—some small, some medium, and a few really tall. None was the Royce Vase. He didn't see a single can of paint.

Dink decided to look for books about old silver and found a fat one. He flipped through the pages and saw pictures of silver bowls, candlesticks, pitchers, and belt buckles. Checking the index, he found the pages about Paul Revere. He turned to that chapter and found photos of several tall vases. One of them could have been the vase Foley Royce's ancestor had bought.

Dink closed the book and returned it to the shelf. Was this where Maria found the picture to send to Kip?

The bottom shelf was filled with books about famous people who were no longer alive. There was one about President John F. Kennedy. Dink ran a finger along the book spines: Elvis Presley. Abraham Lincoln. Marilyn Monroe. Albert Einstein. Thomas Alva Edison.

"No Royce Vase and no paint," Josh said as he walked into the living room.

"How about cookies?" Dink asked him.

Josh grinned. "Found one, but it's gone now," he said.

Ruth Rose came from the bedroom. "Maria sure has a lot of vases!" she said. "I counted eleven in a cabinet. But none were twenty-one inches high."

The apartment door opened, and Maria came in, out of breath. "Hi, kids," she said. "How have you been entertaining yourselves?"

"Checking out all your books," Dink said. "You must read a lot."

"My favorite hobby," Maria said. "Notice I have no TV!"

She walked over and gave Ruth Rose a hug. "Your gram is still with the police, I'm afraid," she said. "But Lanny is there, too, and they're talking."

"Will she come home tonight?" Ruth Rose asked.

"Honey, I honestly don't know," Maria said. "Lanny promised to call when she knows more, even if it's in the middle of the night."

Dink watched Maria kick off her sneakers and step into pink bunny slippers. *Is this a woman who would leave her best friend in jail?* he wondered.

"You don't have a TV?" Josh asked. "How do you do that?"

"I watch important stuff on my iPad," Maria said. "But I'd rather be out walking or riding my bike than sitting on the sofa. There's a great park not far away, and Green-Wood Cemetery has wonderful walking trails."

"You hike in the cemetery?" Josh asked.

"All the time," Maria said. She winked. "That place is filled with treasures."

Maria cooked spaghetti with turkey meatballs for supper. The kids did the dishes while Maria laid out their sleeping bags. "Do you require stuffed animals to sleep with?" she asked, grinning at the kids.

"Josh has a giraffe named Jerome," Ruth Rose said. "But Dink and I are too mature."

"Jerome Giraffe belongs to one of my little brothers," Josh said.

Dink grinned. "Then why is Jerome always on your bed?" he asked.

"Because I feed him cookies!" Josh said.

Maria pulled a small wooden chest from behind one of the sofas. "Here's a stash of my grandkids' favorite books," she said. "Help yourselves if you want something to read. I have a date with Bertie."

"Who's Bertie?" Josh asked.

"Bertie is my nickname for Albert Einstein," Maria said, pulling the man's biography from the bottom shelf. "Einstein's sister was called Maria, like me. I think my parents named me after her. If I'd been a boy, they'd have named me Albert."

CHAPTER 12

Josh and Ruth Rose each chose a book from the box. Dink took the Thomas Edison biography from the bookshelf.

Josh went into the bathroom with his backpack and came out wearing Batman pajamas. He climbed into his sleeping bag, then hopped right out again. He turned around and reached his arm all the way to the end of the bag. "There's something in here," he muttered.

"Probably a tarantula," Dink said. "They hide in dark places and wait for their prey."

"Nope, it's a lollipop!" Josh said.

"Are you going to eat that?" Dink asked. "It might have been down there for years."

Josh crawled into the bag again and set the lollipop next to the lamp on a table. "Maybe I will, Bill." Three minutes later, Josh was asleep.

Dink read about how Thomas Alva Edison invented the electric lightbulb and other things. When his eyes got tired, he closed them. He thought about what life was like before electricity. No computers. No TV. People lit candles or kerosene lamps. He shuddered, remembering the darkness when they were locked inside the crypt. Good thing that jogger came along.

Dink opened his eyes. Yeah, that jogger let them out, but who locked them *in*? Maybe a breeze did close the door, making that hasp thing fall over the metal loop. But who put the stick through the loop? Could it really have been a parakeet?

Dink shook his head. It was hard to believe a parakeet could jam a stick through that small loop with its beak. It must have been a person. Would someone just passing by do it? Maybe that guy mowing the lawn noticed the plastic tie had been cut. Maybe he shoved a stick through the hasp to keep the door from opening until he got a new padlock.

Dink closed his eyes again, picturing the guy with the lawn mower. He had looked at them funny when they asked about the Royce crypt. He had a name tag on his shirt. What was it? Alan? Alfred? No, it was Albert. Like Albert Einstein.

Maria called Albert Einstein *Bertie.* The name Bertie clicked in Dink's brain. Where had he heard it today? He let his mind take him backward. They were on the train. Then they met Ruth Rose's gram. They took a taxi to Park Slope. They stopped by Kip's Place. Josh joked about the old gravestone, and Kip said his cousin had found it somewhere. His cousin *Bertie.*

Dink sat up in his sleeping bag. The Edison book slipped to the floor. *Bertie* was a nickname for *Albert. Could Albert who works in Green-Wood Cemetery be Kip's cousin Bertie?*

Dink's mind raced. Albert could get the keys to the crypts. Albert might also have the key to Kip's studio.

Maybe *Albert* stole the Royce Vase, not Maria.

Dink turned to Ruth Rose's sleeping

bag. Only the top of her hair stuck out of the bag. The book she had been reading lay on the floor.

Dink poked her awake, then did the same to Josh. They stared at him with sleepy eyes.

"Is it morning?" Ruth Rose asked.

"I think I know who stole the Royce Vase," Dink said.

"You said it was Maria," Josh mumbled.

"I know I did, but now I have a different idea," Dink said.

Ruth Rose sat up. "Who do you think stole it?" she asked.

"Albert," Dink said.

"Who's Albert?" Josh asked.

"The guy in the cemetery," Dink told him. "He was mowing the grass. We asked him how to find the crypt."

"But how would he know my grandmother made a vase, and how would he steal it?" Ruth Rose asked.

"Because maybe Albert is Bertie," Dink said.

"Who's Bertie?" Josh asked. "I'm confused."

"Remember that gravestone we saw at Kip's?" Dink asked.

"Yeah, gross," Josh said.

"Kip told us his cousin Bertie gave it to him," Dink went on.

He explained why he thought Kip's cousin Bertie and Albert, the cemetery guy, were the same person. "If Albert is Kip's cousin, he might have seen your grandmother's vase when he visited the art studio. And he could get the key to the studio from Kip. Albert could also get keys to the crypts, since he works at the cemetery. Maybe he goes inside the crypts and takes pictures of the stuff he sees, like the Royce Vase. If I'm right, *Albert* gave Kip the vase photo that's tacked up in the studio. And I think Albert stole Ruth Rose's grandmother's vase, and broke the bathroom window to make Kip think some burglar did it."

"So it was Albert who took Gram Hathaway's vase into the crypt and switched it for the Royce Vase?" Josh asked.

"That makes a lot more sense than Maria doing it," Dink said.

"Or my grandmother!" Ruth Rose said.

"Plus, I think Albert might have locked us in the crypt," Dink went on. "The wind could have blown the door shut, but the wind didn't jam a stick so the door wouldn't open."

"Why would he do that?" Ruth Rose asked.

"It makes sense," Josh said before Dink could answer. "If he did steal the Royce Vase, he wouldn't want us poking around in there, would he? I mean, if we found a clue, he wouldn't want us going to the cops."

They looked at each other. Josh gulped. "Maybe he was going to leave us in there," he whispered. "Forever. Our bones would be—"

"Don't talk about skeletons in the middle of the night, okay, Josh?" Ruth Rose said. She pushed her hair out of her eyes. "If Albert still has the Royce Vase and we can find it, they'll have to let Gram come home!"

"How would we find it?" Dink asked. "He probably stashed it away somewhere until he has time to sell it."

"If I were him, I'd hide it where no one would ever look," Ruth Rose said.

"Where?" Josh asked.

"If Albert has keys to the other crypts in the cemetery," she whispered, "maybe he hid it inside a different crypt!"

CHAPTER 13

Josh let out a hoot. "There's no way you're getting me back in one of those crypts," he said.

"Not *one* crypt," Ruth Rose said, grinning. "There are at least a hundred in the cemetery. We have to search all of them!"

"I don't think Albert would hide the vase inside a crypt," Dink said. "He'd be afraid some family member would show up and find the Royce Vase in their crypt. Nobody expected Foley Royce to visit his family crypt, but he did."

"You're right," Josh said. "So that leaves . . . the rest of the planet."

The kids lay back in their sleeping bags. Dink thought about where Albert would hide a valuable stolen vase.

Ruth Rose thought about her grandmother.

"You know what I don't understand?" Josh said in the darkness.

"Anything?" Dink joked.

"No, seriously," Josh said, sitting up. "I get that Albert might have snuck into Kip's and stolen Gram's vase, then switched it for the Royce Vase. Maybe he hid the Royce Vase someplace and locked us in the crypt."

"So what don't you understand?" Ruth Rose asked.

"At first, Kip agreed your gram's vase was broken in the kiln," Josh said. "But later he told us it was stolen *out of the kiln.* Why did Kip change his story?"

"Because he found the smashed window and some other things got stolen," Ruth Rose said. "He told us that."

"You know what *I* don't get?" Dink added. "How did Albert know your gram's vase was *in* the kiln? And how did he get it out of the kiln? Kip kept it locked."

Nobody had an answer.

"Anyway," Ruth Rose said, "we have to prove Albert really is Kip's cousin. Then we have to find the vase and prove Albert stole it."

"Oh, that should be easy," Josh said, sticking the lollipop in his mouth.

Dink shut off the light. "I have a plan," he said after a few minutes.

"What's the plan, Dan?" Josh asked. "No more cemeteries, I hope."

"We search Kip's Place," Dink said.

"Why there?" Ruth Rose asked.

"Because I think Albert would hide the Royce Vase somewhere he could get to it easily," Dink answered. "The perfect hiding place would be at Cousin Kip's shop. Kip wouldn't know it was there, and Albert could get the vase whenever he wanted to."

"So we tell Kip we think his cousin is a crook and we want to search his shop?" Josh said. "That should go over big."

"No, we don't tell Kip until we can prove it," Dink said. "We just snoop around."

"I like the snooping part," Ruth Rose said.

"So where will Kip be while we're snooping?" Josh asked.

"Not you," Dink said. "Ruth Rose and I will search while you keep Kip busy."

"Busy how? And why do you guys get to do the fun part?" Josh asked.

"You'll have fun, too," Dink said. "You'll be doing an art project."

Josh pulled the lollipop from his mouth. "What kind of art project?" he asked.

"Ask Kip to show you how to do a gravestone rubbing," Dink said. "While he's doing that, we snoop!"

"But I hate gravestones, and I don't want to rub one!" Josh cried.

"You don't really rub it," Ruth Rose said. "You put a paper over the gravestone, then rub the paper with a crayon. The letters come through onto the paper. It's cool!"

"But while I'm playing with crayons, Kip will see you guys wandering around," Josh said.

"No, he won't. The gravestone is on

the sidewalk. Kip will be with you, and we'll be inside," Dink said. "Just make sure not to learn too fast. Keep his attention on you while we—"

"Snoop," Josh said.

"Try to help my grandmother," Ruth Rose said.

Josh let out a big sigh. "Okay, when do we do this?" he asked.

Dink checked the time on his phone. "It's ten p.m.," he said. "How about after breakfast?"

CHAPTER 14

"Wakey-wakey, darlings!" Maria called. She was in the kitchen, wearing an apron with a yellow smiley face. "If you don't come and eat these pancakes, I'll have to feed them to the pigeons!"

"No, please don't do that!" Josh said as he struggled out of his sleeping bag. His hair stuck up like wires.

"Okay, but go wash first," Maria said.

Josh ran into the bathroom while Dink and Ruth Rose rolled up the sleeping bags.

A few minutes later, they all sat at the table. They helped themselves to pancakes, syrup, and sliced bananas.

"How did you sleep?" Maria asked. "Was the floor too hard?"

"It was like camping!" Ruth Rose said. "My little brother and I sleep on the ground outside every summer."

"Josh had bad dreams," Dink said. "He kept saying 'I miss my giraffe!' "

"Did not," said Josh.

Maria put her plate in the sink. "I'm going to the police station," she said, placing two keys on the counter. "The big key opens the door downstairs. The small, shiny one is for my front door."

"Say hi to Gram!" Ruth Rose said.

"I'll do better than that!" Maria said. "With Lanny's help, I'll bring her home!"

The kids cleaned up the table, brushed their teeth, and headed out the door.

"So how do we work Operation Josh?" Josh asked.

"Who named it that?" Ruth Rose asked.

Josh grinned. "I did," he said. "Since

you get to search, I get to call it after myself."

"Okay," Dink said. "Remember: when we get there, you ask Kip to teach you how to do a gravestone rubbing."

Five minutes later, they stopped in front of the dry cleaner's. "What happens if you find it?" Josh asked. "The Royce Vase."

"We show it to Kip," Dink said. "That's when we tell him his cousin Albert stole it."

"And we text Maria at the police station," Ruth Rose said. "She'll tell the cops we found the vase. They'll arrest Albert and let Gram go!"

The kids stepped into Kip's Place. No one was there, not even Kip.

"He's not here," Josh whispered. "We can—"

Just then, Kip stepped through the door with the PRIVATE sign. "Hi again," he said. "What's going on?"

Dink gave Josh a little push. "Josh has something to ask you," he said. "Right, Josh?"

Josh put on his biggest smile. "You know that gravestone thing you have outside?" he said. "Can you teach me how to do a rubbing? I'd really like to learn, so I can show my art teacher in Connecticut."

Kip stared at the kids. "Sure thing," he said after a minute. "How about you two? Want to learn, too?"

"We'll just watch," Dink said. "We're terrible at art, right, Ruth Rose?"

"Right," Ruth Rose said. "Awful."

Kip pulled a large sheet of paper from a box standing in a corner. He grabbed a few thick crayons, a roll of tape, and a damp sponge. "Let's go outside," he said.

The gravestone was leaning against one corner of his building. The sun shone on the stone's markings, but they were too faint to read. "This thing is about one hundred years old, so first we clean it,"

Kip said, handing the sponge to Josh. "Pat it gently. Try to get the dirt out of all the grooves."

Dink wondered why Kip wasn't wearing his purple sunglasses. The sun was bright as it reflected off the sidewalk and window glass.

Josh did a good job wiping the gravestone, turning the sponge black.

"Great," Kip said. "Next, we tape this paper over the stone." He did that, smoothing the paper with his hands. "The rest is easy. You just scribble the crayon over the paper. What color?"

Josh chose a blue crayon. Kip showed him how to hold it sideways. "Don't rub too hard," he said.

Josh began moving the crayon across the paper. Immediately, some bumpy blue impressions appeared. "Cool!" he said.

"Um, Kip, may I use your bathroom?" Dink asked.

"Sure, and the window is fixed," Kip said. "You know where it is, right?"

Dink nodded and walked inside. Instead of heading straight to the restroom, he stopped in the art room, checking the shelves and corners for a tall silver vase. Feeling nervous, he peeked behind canvases and under tables. He even stuck his arm into a trash can filled with paper. No vase.

He walked down the hall to the

bathroom. The window had new glass, and the floor had been swept clean. There was a cabinet under the sink, so Dink opened it. He saw rolls of toilet paper and a bottle of glass cleaner. No vase here, either.

Dink ran back to the art room. Kip had left the door with the PRIVATE sign partly open, so he stepped inside. He eyed the drawers in Kip's desk, but decided they were too small to hide a vase nearly two feet tall.

The desktop held a laptop and printer, a cell phone, and a tray holding pens, paper clips, and two pennies. There was no window, but a desk lamp lit the room.

A mirror hung on the wall over the desk. Dink glanced in the glass and saw his own sweaty face and blue eyes. Behind him was a bookshelf against the wall. The five shelves held a bunch of small clay animals.

Dink turned to look at them. He saw

ducks, pigs, cats, and dogs. One dog with floppy ears reminded Dink of Josh's basset hound, Pal. Then he noticed something behind the dog. A round object caught the lamp's reflection.

He looked closer, then slid the dog to the right and saw a doorknob. *Weird place for a doorknob,* Dink thought. Then he realized the bookshelf was built onto a door.

Dink looked over his shoulder to make sure he was alone. He reached for the doorknob and turned it. He heard a click, and the bookshelf quietly moved toward him. On the other side of the door was a closet with more shelves. With the door shelf closed, no one would ever know there was a secret room.

Dink stared with his mouth open. On a shelf two feet from his nose stood the Royce Vase. Even he could tell the vase was real silver, not painted. It gleamed from the lamplight coming over Dink's

shoulder. The vase resembled some he'd seen in Maria's book, and was exactly like the photo in Kip's art room.

Then he saw something that made him nod and take a picture with his phone. He pushed the bookshelf closed and heard the latch click.

When he turned to leave, he nearly bumped into Kip.

CHAPTER 15

Kip was standing in the office doorway. Josh stood behind him, holding his art paper covered with blue crayon marks. Ruth Rose was behind Josh with her eyes wide.

"Did you get lost?" Kip asked Dink. "This isn't the bathroom." He was smiling, but with his mouth only. His eyes were light brown and staring. They reminded Dink of a snake's eyes he'd seen on TV. The guy on the show said snakes couldn't blink because they had no eyelids.

Dink did blink, and he tried to smile back at Kip. "Yeah, I found it," he said.

"When I came out, I noticed these cool clay animals." He held up his phone. "I wanted to get a picture."

"Did you get it?" Kip asked. "The picture?" He nodded toward Dink's phone.

"No," Dink said. He tapped on the camera icon and held his phone out to Kip. "Would you take one of me in front of them?" He stepped to the side, hoping his body was blocking the secret doorknob.

Kip took the phone and aimed it at Dink's face. "Smile," he said. "Don't look so scared."

Dink grinned as Kip took the picture. "Want another, just in case?" Kip asked.

"No, thanks. We, um, have to get going," Dink said. "Maria's expecting us."

"Look!" Josh said. He held up his rubbing. "This gravestone was for some guy named Donald Skane. He died in 1920!"

"That's why my cousin Bertie brought it to me," Kip said. "Same last name as ours, but no relation to us."

DONALD SKANE
BORN 1835
DIED 1920

"Does your cousin work in a cemetery?" Ruth Rose asked. "Is his name Albert?"

Kip nodded. "Yes, but we call him Bertie," he said. "He's a groundskeeper at Green-Wood. He finds all kinds of stuff."

The kids moved back into the art room. Kip closed the door to his office. "Say hi to your grandmother," he said to Ruth Rose. "I mean, is she still . . . ?"

"She'll be home today," Ruth Rose said. "Maybe."

Kip took Josh's rubbing and laid it across a worktable. Then he chose a can from a shelf. "Step back. This is a fixative, and you do not want to inhale the fumes," Kip said. "It smells nasty, but it'll keep the crayon from rubbing off." He sprayed the smelly mist on the blue markings before rolling the paper into a tube. He slipped a rubber band around the tube and handed it to Josh. "Good to show your teacher."

The kids thanked Kip and left. They passed the sandwich shop and waved through the window at Simon.

"Well, we didn't find a silver vase worth a jillion dollars," Josh said. "But I got a piece of paper with crayon marks on it!"

"Who says we didn't find the vase?" Dink asked. He held up his phone and wiggled it. "Wait till you see!"

They walked to a bench near a statue of a soldier on a horse. Dink sat between Josh and Ruth Rose and opened up his photos. There was the picture Kip had just taken: Dink standing in front of the clay animals.

"Why do you look like you've just seen a ghost?" Ruth Rose asked.

"Wait," Dink said, swiping back to the previous picture. "Take a look!"

It was the photo of the Royce Vase inside the hidden closet.

"Holy hippos!" Josh said. "You found it!"

Lined up on the other shelves were candlesticks, small statues, bowls, and more vases. Dink counted almost fifty items.

"Everything looks old and expensive!" Ruth Rose said.

The bottom shelf held three small panels made of stained glass. They were dusty, and the wood frames were scratched. Dink thought they looked like one of the pictures in an art book at Maria's apartment.

"What is all that stuff?" Josh asked.

Dink explained how he had found the closet. "I'll bet these things were all stolen from other crypts in the cemetery," he said.

"Amazing!" Ruth Rose said. "So Albert hid this stuff behind that door, and Kip never knew!"

"Wait," Dink said. He made the picture bigger and pointed to the shelf next to the Royce Vase. "See that?" He moved his finger to something small, flat, and purple.

Josh and Ruth Rose leaned closer.

"I give up," Josh said.

"Those are Kip's purple sunglasses," Dink said. "He wasn't wearing them when you guys were doing the rubbing, even though it was bright outside. That's because he'd left them in the secret closet.

He must have forgotten them. Anyway, this proves Kip knew what was hidden in the closet. I think Kip is the crook!"

"Kip? But I thought it was Albert!" Ruth Rose said.

Dink sat back on the bench. "Albert and Kip must do it together," he said. "I think Albert gets keys to the crypts and snoops around inside. If he finds expensive stuff like the Royce Vase, he texts pictures to Kip. Then Kip makes the fakes to switch for the real stuff."

"Or he gets someone else to make a fake," Ruth Rose said. "Like my grandmother!"

"Clever!" Josh said. "If they put a fake Royce Vase in the crypt, no one would ever realize the real one was gone. Even if someone from the family went inside the crypt."

"Kip probably got his cousin Albert to sneak your grandmother's vase into the crypt," Dink said to Ruth Rose. "He works in the cemetery, so no one would notice him hanging around."

"At least we have proof Gram didn't do it!" Ruth Rose said. "We can show this picture to the cops!"

Dink tapped Ruth Rose's backpack. "Does your guidebook tell how to get to the police station?" he asked.

CHAPTER 16

Twenty minutes later, the kids were sitting in a small room at the Park Slope police station. They sat facing Officer Pete Foster, who was behind his desk with Dink's phone in front of him.

"Well, I'll be darned," Officer Foster said. He was staring at Dink's photo of the Royce Vase.

Minutes earlier, he had texted the photo to Foley Royce, asking, *"This item just recovered. Is it Royce Vase?"*

The answer came back quickly: *"Yes! When can I get it?"*

Officer Foster responded, *"You can*

pick it up at the police station at your convenience."

Dink had explained about meeting Albert in the cemetery, and how they'd been locked in the crypt. He told Officer Foster how they figured out that Albert, who mowed the lawns in Green-Wood Cemetery, was Kip's cousin Bertie.

"My grandmother copied her vase from a picture Kip has in his shop," Ruth Rose told the officer. "We think Kip's cousin texted him that picture from inside the crypt. Later, Kip or Albert went back to the crypt and switched Gram's vase for the Royce Vase!"

Officer Foster stood up. He took out his phone and texted Officer Deming, *On our way. Pick up Albert Skane at Green-Wood.* "Okay, now let's go talk to these naughty cousins."

The three kids rode in the back of Officer Foster's cruiser. He pulled up at Kip's Place just as Officer Deming stopped at

the dry cleaner's. They watched Albert climb out of the backseat of her cruiser.

"This should be interesting," Officer Foster said. "Let's go inside, kids."

Kip greeted them all. "Hello, Officers. Hi, kids. What's going on?" he asked. Then he noticed his cousin. "Yo, Bertie? What's up?"

"We have reason to believe you're in possession of a stolen vase," Officer Foster said. He opened Dink's phone and showed the picture of the Royce Vase in the secret closet. "This one. Does it look familiar, sir?"

Kip stared at the phone. He shook his head. "I have no idea what that is," he said. "Maybe my cousin does, but I—"

"Don't lie!" Albert burst out. "I helped you build those shelves! You know darned well what it is!"

Officers Foster and Deming led Kip and his cousin into the office. Dink showed them the secret doorknob behind the clay dog.

Officer Foster opened the door and whistled. "Your scheme is over, gentlemen," he said. He pointed to Kip's sunglasses next to the vase. "Those are your glasses, right? Your fingerprints will be all over the Royce Vase there, right?"

"It was all his idea!" Kip said, pointing at his cousin.

"Like heck it was!" Albert shouted. "You asked me if I could get keys to the crypts. I saved all your texts!"

"We'd love to read those texts, and we will," Officer Deming said. "But let's continue this down at the station." The officers handcuffed Kip and Albert and took them outside to the cruisers.

Officer Deming put her arm around Ruth Rose's shoulders. "I'll bring your grandmother back to Ms. Hoffman's apartment in half an hour," she said.

Dink called Maria and told her the news. She said she'd order a couple of pizzas.

Now they were all sitting around her table, eating and laughing.

Gram's vase stood on the coffee table next to the pizza box.

"It's not very pretty, is it?" Gram said.

"I think it's beautiful!" Maria said. "And if it could talk, what a story it would tell!"

Gram told them about her stay at the police station. "They put me in a room with a bed and small bathroom," she said. "That nice Officer Deming brought me tea and cookies."

"The crypt was worse!" Josh said. "Dink and Ruth Rose were scared because of the dead body under the floor, but I told them not to worry."

"Oh yeah?" Dink said. "Did I forget to tell you I recorded everything you said inside the crypt?" He pulled out his phone. "Want to listen, Josh?"

Josh reached for a slice of pizza. "No, thanks," he said.

Dink grinned. "Just kidding. I didn't record anything," he said. "Remember, my phone battery was down. I was plenty scared in the crypt. I almost fainted when the door slammed!"

"And I was terrified!" Ruth Rose admitted. "I still have goose bumps!"

Josh grinned at Dink and Ruth Rose. "You guys are so cool," he said.

"We know, Joe," Ruth Rose said.

DID YOU FIND THE
SECRET MESSAGE
HIDDEN IN THIS BOOK?

If you *don't* want
to know the answer,
don't look at the bottom
of this page!

GET THE FACTS FROM A TO Z!

To learn more about the facts in this mystery, find these books at your local library or bookstore:

Books About New York City
> *Kidding Around NYC: For Kids Who Want the Inside Track on the City* by Suzanne Roche (Oak Lei, 2015)
> *This Is New York* by Miroslav Sasek (Universe, 2003; originally published in 1960)

Books About Famous Cemeteries
> *Rest in Peace: A History of American Cemeteries* by Meg Greene (Twenty-First Century, 2008)

Books About Parrots and Parakeets
> *Parrots* by Ruth Bjorklund (Scholastic, 2012)
> *Pet Parakeets* by Julia Barnes (Gareth Stevens, 2006)

Books About Pottery
> *Ceramics for Kids: Creative Clay Projects to Pinch, Roll, Coil, Slam & Twist* by Mary Ellis (Lark, 2004)

The Kids 'N' Clay Ceramics Book: Handbuilding and Wheel-Throwing Projects from the Kids 'N' Clay Pottery Studio (Tricycle, 2000)

Books About Stained Glass

Crafting with Kids by Jennifer Casa (Visual, 2011)

Crafting with Tissue Paper by Kathleen Petelinsek (Cherry Lake, 2014)

Mason Jar Crafts for Kids: More than 25 Cool, Crafty Projects to Make for Your Friends, Your Family, and Yourself! by Linda Braden (Sky Pony, 2015)

Books About Rubbings

Fun and Festive Fall Crafts: Leaf Rubbings, Dancing Scarecrows, and Pinecone Turkeys by Randel McGee (Enslow Elementary, 2014)

Making Paper & Fabric Rubbings: Capturing Designs from Brasses, Gravestones, Carved Doors, Coins & More by Cecily Barth Firestein (Lark, 2001)

A TO Z MYSTERIES® fans, check out Ron Roy's other great mystery series!

Capital Mysteries

#1: Who Cloned the President?
#2: Kidnapped at the Capital
#3: The Skeleton in the Smithsonian
#4: A Spy in the White House
#5: Who Broke Lincoln's Thumb?
#6: Fireworks at the FBI
#7: Trouble at the Treasury
#8: Mystery at the Washington Monument
#9: A Thief at the National Zoo
#10: The Election-Day Disaster
#11: The Secret at Jefferson's Mansion
#12: The Ghost at Camp David
#13: Trapped on the D.C. Train!
#14: Turkey Trouble on the National Mall

January Joker
February Friend
March Mischief
April Adventure
May Magic
June Jam
July Jitters
August Acrobat
September Sneakers
October Ogre
November Night
December Dog
New Year's Eve Thieves